D1326430

The
Frost
Goblin

For Coco,
who is every bit as fabulous as Ada Frostgobble – A.E.

For all the quiet Berties – F.W.

SIMON & SCHUSTER

First published in Great Britain in 2022 by Simon & Schuster UK Ltd • 1st Floor, 222 Gray's Inn Road, London WC1X 8HB • Text copyright © 2022 Abi Elphinstone Illustrations copyright © 2022 Fiona Woodcock • The right of Abi Elphinstone and Fiona Woodcock to be identified as the author and illustrator of this work has been asserted by them in accordance with the Copyright, Designs and Patents Act, 1988 • All rights reserved, including the right of reproduction in whole or in part in any form • A CIP catalogue record for this book is available from the British Library upon request • ISBN: 978-1-4711-9981-3 (HB) ISBN: 978-1-4711-9982-0 (eBook) • Printed in China • 10 9 8 7 6 5 4 3 2 1

FSC
www.fsc.org

MIX
Paper from
responsible sources
FSC® C144853

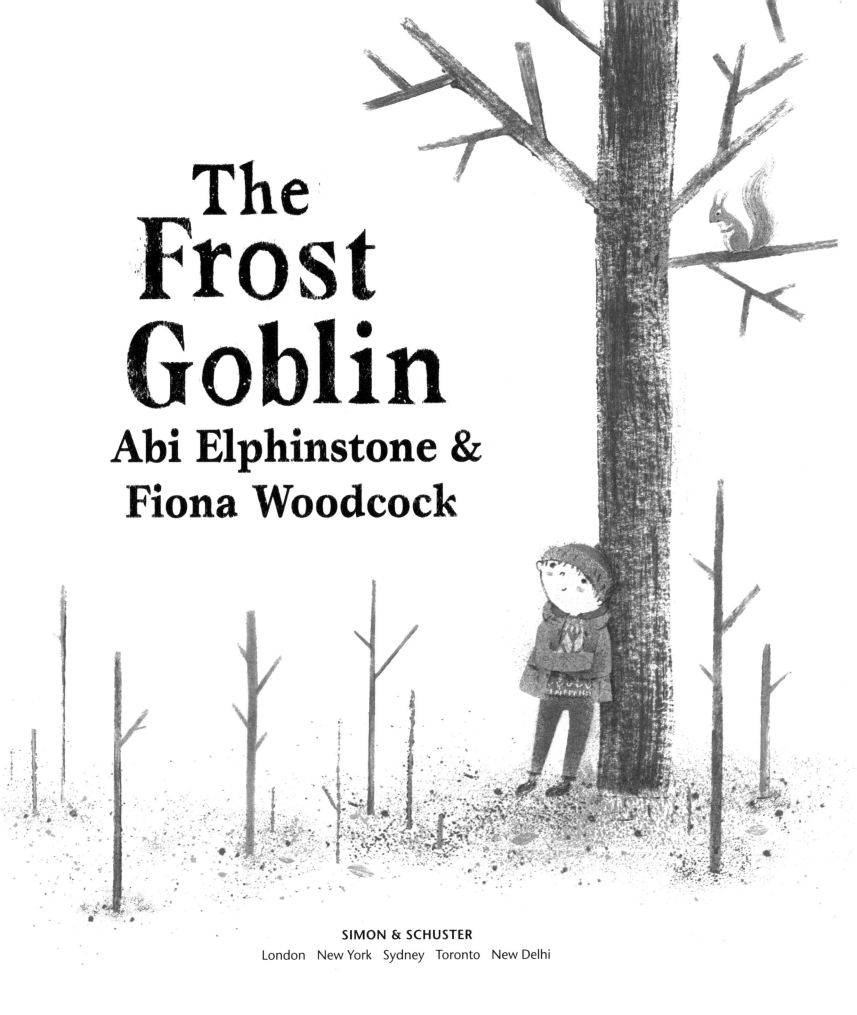

The Frost Goblin

Abi Elphinstone &
Fiona Woodcock

SIMON & SCHUSTER
London   New York   Sydney   Toronto   New Delhi

Stories, like children, never sit still. And the story
I am about to tell you is one of the most fidgety of all.
It is the story of the deepest frost of the year. The one
that tiptoes into your garden in the middle of the night
and turns your whole world silver. The one that,
if scattered in just the right way, sparks magic.

Some people say that behind all this lies the mischief-maker, Jack Frost. But tales of him arrived long after the very first story about frost had twisted and turned and changed shape entirely. You see, the real story has nothing to do with Jack Frost. And everything to do with goblins . . .

Bertie Crash-Wallop, of 33 Muddle Lane, sat cross-legged under the kitchen table with his hands over his ears. It was Friday evening and dinner was over. He'd made it through another week. Possibly the loudest one yet.

His older sisters, eleven-year-old triplets known in school as The Hurricane, had recently joined the debating club and they had loud views on absolutely everything. Tonight they were arguing about what laws they'd introduce if they were prime minister: homework-free birthdays, school trips to space and the immediate banning of broccoli. And they weren't the only ones making a racket in the kitchen. Bertie's mother was a singer, the best their little town of Clatterstomp had ever seen, and she was warbling her way through a crossword. Bertie's father, meanwhile – a sports teacher at the local primary school – was refereeing The Hurricane's argument, whistle and all.

Bertie kept his hands firmly over his ears. At seven years old, he had come to the gloomy conclusion that there must have been a mix-up in the hospital when he was born and that he had found his way into the Crash-Wallop family by mistake. He wasn't loud like his sisters and parents. He was quiet. Very quiet. In fact, whole weekends could pass without him saying a single word. And sometimes this left Bertie feeling rather lonely and sad, as if he didn't quite belong.

Indeed he was starting to wonder whether his family knew even the most basic things about him.

Like the fact that his favourite breakfast was pancakes heaped with blueberries and honey, with a banana milkshake on the side.

Every now and again, Bertie felt so out of place, and so awfully alone, his heart wobbled and he felt the need to leave the house completely. And so it happened that while the debating raged, the refereeing ramped up and the warbling reached its crescendo, Bertie shuffled out from beneath the kitchen table, slipped on his warmest coat and stole into the garden.

It was dark outside and the December air was so cold it stung Bertie's cheeks. For a while he simply sat on the swing watching the moon. It was round and bright and it hung in the sky like a giant marble.

It was the sort of moon, Bertie thought, that looked as if it might have secrets.

The silhouette of an owl glided across it and Bertie felt his eyes drawn to the wall that separated his family's garden from the one next door. It was just a wall covered in ivy but as Bertie looked, he couldn't help thinking there might be a bit more to it. The moonlight throbbed and Bertie blinked. Halfway up the wall, almost lost in the ivy, was something small, black and round. Bertie stood up and took a step closer. Then he frowned.

It was a door handle. One he had never noticed before.

Bertie pulled the ivy back and his toes tingled, the way toes sometimes do when they sense an adventure unfolding. Before him was a very old, very small wooden door.

"Grown-ups would struggle to fit through this," Bertie muttered, "but seven-year-olds . . ."

And because the rest of the Crash-Wallops were making such a racket inside, nobody heard the little door in the wall creak open as Bertie stepped over the threshold.

The neighbouring garden was a jungle of weeds and brambles. Number 35 Muddle Lane had been 'FOR SALE' for as long as Bertie could remember. He often saw people arrive in Clatterstomp to look round it, but nobody seemed to buy it. And so, year after year, it lay empty. At least Bertie had always assumed that it was empty.

Until now.

From a thicket of weeds in front of the house came three unexpected noises. First, a sniff. Next a *hmmmmm*. Then, finally, the sound of someone whispering: "Yes, tonight is the night!"

Bertie edged backwards. He was starting to feel ever so slightly afraid. But as he moved, a twig beneath his shoe snapped.

There was a gasp from the thicket. And then, something the size of a child but very much not one – for children do not have large, pointed ears, bulbous noses and hairy feet – darted out from the undergrowth, yanked open the back door of Number 35 and disappeared inside.

Bertie shook his head in disbelief, and that could well have been the end of that had it not been for Bertie's toes. These toes realised the adventure was now in full swing and quite independently of Bertie himself, they spurred him on after the creature until he, too, was charging through the back door of 35 Muddle Lane.

The house was full of shadows. Bertie swallowed his nerves and followed the sound of scampering footsteps down a corridor into a kitchen. And it was there, in the light cast by the street lamp outside, that his eyes fell upon the most extraordinary sight.

Not only did the creature have large, pointed ears, a bulbous nose and hairy feet, but in the lamplight, he could see that it also had green skin. And it was wearing dungarees.

Now, there is a tipping point in every adventure —
a point where you either feel too frightened to go on or
too curious to turn back. Bertie looked his tipping point
in the eye and decided to go on.

"What— what are you?" he whispered, inching nearer.

The creature shrieked, then flung open a cupboard
door beneath the sink, wriggled through it and promptly
vanished from sight.

Bertie peered into the cupboard. It was empty. Then he
noticed the trapdoor. His heart quickened as he pulled
it open. A flight of soily stairs wound downwards and
Bertie's heart beat faster still because he knew now that he
was on the edge of something astonishing. He tiptoed down
a few steps and what he saw next took his breath away.

There was a family living at 35 Muddle Lane.
Only they didn't live in the house itself. They lived under
it, in a magnificent cave lit by fireflies. The cave was
the size of a cathedral and lined with silver trees that
grew around a glimmering silver lake. In amongst these
trees, on the far side of the lake, were three hammocks
laden with quilts and dozens of branches hollowed out
to hold row upon row of books. Bertie crept down the
rest of the stairs and made his way through the silver
trees, following the unexpected but unmistakable smell
of melted chocolate.

From somewhere up ahead, there was a gasp. And then
the words: "Archibald Frostgobble, what have you done?!"

Bertie froze. This was the kind of voice his mother used at teatime when she wanted vegetables eaten: stern, but also rather fed up. And yet Bertie went on again, ever more curious, until the trees parted before the lake and he came to a table piled high with every kind of freshly-made fudge you could imagine: blueberry cubes dusted with coconut; mint cubes with swirls of chocolate; red-and-white striped cubes that might have been rhubarb-and-custard flavoured; and toffee cubes crammed with nuts.

Mr Frostgobble, the creature Bertie had followed, was perched on an armchair on one side of this table. And opposite him, stirring a cauldron full of chocolate fudge, stood Mrs Frostgobble. She was as green as her husband, with the same pointed ears, bulbous nose and hairy feet. At the sight of Bertie, she clutched her wooden spoon to her chest.

Mr Frostgobble winced. "I went Upstairs to sniff the night, Florence – to see how much frost would be needed later on. And there he was, standing in the garden!" He cast Bertie a nervous look. "I thought you said children these days weren't that curious!"

Mrs Frostgobble gripped her spoon. "Well, this one certainly is!"

"We should tell him to leave," Mr Frostgobble whispered. "Goblins and children don't mix well."

Bertie's eyebrows shot up. "Goblins? But– but I thought goblins belonged in fairy tales . . . "

Mrs Frostgobble looked rather hurt. "And in caves under kitchen sinks where trees are made of moonlight, lakes are filled with molten stardust and cauldrons conjure unlimited fudge, because that is all we goblins eat."

Mr Frostgobble grimaced in Bertie's direction. "What if he tells his parents what he's seen?"

"You don't need to worry about me," Bertie cut in. "No-one at home listens to what I have to say anyway."

Mr Frostgobble turned to his wife. "Even if he doesn't snitch on us, we need to get him out of the way because up in the garden I smelt the chill of winter's coldest night approaching."

Mrs Frostgobble's eyes widened. "The deepest, most important frost of the year – we're to scatter it tonight?!"

Her husband nodded. "And we have the entire town to get round before dawn breaks if the frost is to work its magic! Lawns, leaves, lamp posts, letterboxes. The whole of Clatterstomp must be covered!"

"You scatter our frost?" Bertie murmured.

Mr Frostgobble raised a green eyebrow at Bertie. "Florence and I have a very busy night ahead of us and what we don't need is a hundred and one questions from you."

Mrs Frostgobble looked at Bertie and then her bulbous nose started wiggling. Up and down, left then right. "We goblins sense all sorts of things in our noses. They wiggle when we're hungry, when we're tired and when we're facing something important. And right now my nose appears to be telling me a significant fact: you are the sort of boy who keeps secrets, rather than spills them. Is that correct?"

"Yes," Bertie replied. And then he added, sadly: "I don't have anyone to spill secrets to."

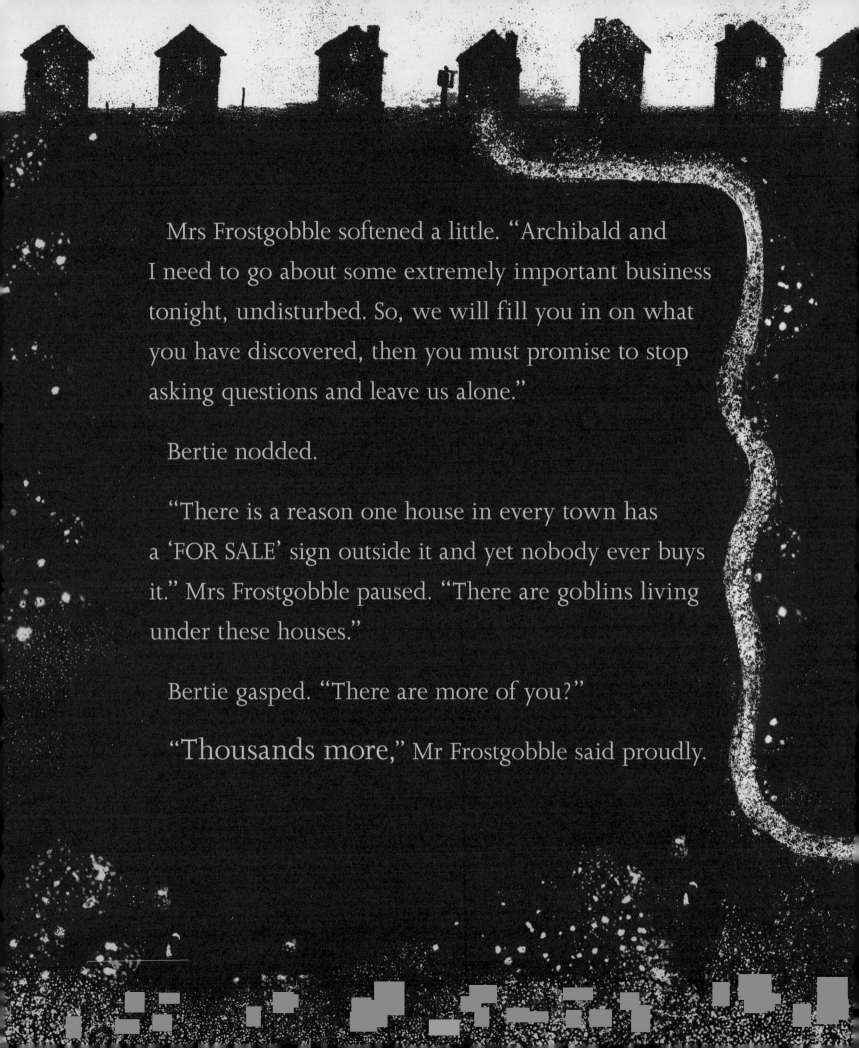

Mrs Frostgobble softened a little. "Archibald and
I need to go about some extremely important business
tonight, undisturbed. So, we will fill you in on what
you have discovered, then you must promise to stop
asking questions and leave us alone."

Bertie nodded.

"There is a reason one house in every town has
a 'FOR SALE' sign outside it and yet nobody ever buys
it." Mrs Frostgobble paused. "There are goblins living
under these houses."

Bertie gasped. "There are more of you?"

"Thousands more," Mr Frostgobble said proudly.

"We goblins play little pranks on people who look round empty houses so that our homes get left alone. That way we can scatter frost every winter without grown-ups," he tutted, "or meddlesome children poking their noses in and asking questions."

Bertie's face shone. He couldn't decide what was more marvellous: knowing that he lived next to a family of goblins or being part of a conversation where he was listened to.

"Every goblin is born with frost magic inside them," Mrs Frostgobble explained. "And when we're young, that's where this magic stays, watching and waiting."

"When we're fully grown and the magic feels like we're up to the challenge of creeping Upstairs and scattering frost, it settles in our fingers." Mr Frostgobble held up his hands and Bertie noticed his fingertips were silver. "Frost comes easily then. It pours from our fingertips, white and sparkling, like sugar. And experienced goblins like Florence and I can coat every garden in Clatterstomp in a single hour." He paused. "But tonight – winter's coldest night – we goblins are tasked with scattering the deepest, most important frost of the year, and it's a much longer job."

"Why?" Bertie asked.

Mrs Frostgobble took a deep breath. "If scattered perfectly, over absolutely everything in its path, not just gardens, the deepest frost has the power to rekindle hope in anyone who's lost it."

Bertie's eyes grew large. "Frost can do that?"

"This frost can. But it must be scattered before dawn breaks for the magic to work. So, Florence and I need to get going now because Clatterstomp has over a hundred lamp posts, all needing frost, and— "

"Archibald!" Mrs Frostgobble yelped. "My— my fingertips! They're green! Yours, too!"

Mr Frostgobble glanced at his hands and shrieked. "Our magic! Where's it gone?!"

Even Bertie looked confused. "But you had it just a moment ago! I saw it with my own eyes! It— "

Bertie jumped as an icy coldness spread out from his palms, then a tingle skittered down his fingers. His mouth fell open. His fingertips were now bright silver, as if he'd dipped them in moonlight. He stared at the goblins and they stared back at him – and his fingertips.

"Impossible!" cried Mrs Frostgobble.
"Disastrous!" cried Mr Frostgobble.

"Awesome!" cried another voice from the far side of the lake.

A little rowing boat made from bark drifted towards them and Bertie saw that a third goblin was sitting inside it. She was smaller than the other two, but just as green, and she was wearing a brightly-patterned tunic.

"Mum! Dad! My magic has arrived!" the goblin shouted, wiggling her silver fingertips high in the air. "I must be the only seven-year-old goblin to have frost magic, don't you think? It means I can go Upstairs at last!"

"How has this happened?" Mrs Frostgobble cried. "Frost magic settles inside goblins when they're fully grown, not when they're seven!"

Mr Frostgobble turned his trembling hands over. "And it's not supposed to vanish once it's settled! Or spark up in the fingertips of a boy from Upstairs! Unless somehow the frost magic has a plan in all of this . . . ?"

The goblin girl's eyes widened as she took in Bertie, then her boat bumped ashore and she clambered out. She strode towards him with the wild excitement of a seven-year-old on the cusp of adventure.

"Careful, Ada!" Mr Frostgobble cried. "We think he can keep secrets but we haven't worked out much else. For all we know, he could bite."

"I don't bite," Bertie replied. "I don't even speak much." Then he added "usually", for tonight he found he was speaking rather a lot and that was because he was beginning to sense that he might be needed. That he, Bertie Crash-Wallop of Number 33 Muddle Lane, might in fact have an important job to do.

"What if— what if I help scatter the frost tonight," he found himself saying. "I don't have anything else planned, other than brushing my teeth and going to bed. And I doubt my family will even notice I'm gone."

Ada clapped her hands. "We'll do it together and it'll be the finest frost anyone has ever seen!"

"Absolutely not," Mrs Frostgobble cried. "You're far too young – and precious – to be gallivanting about Upstairs without your father or me!"

"You could come with us," Bertie ventured, for he couldn't help thinking that wielding magic might require some sort of grown-up supervision.

Mr Frostgobble rolled his eyes. "Goblins can only venture Upstairs if they have magic inside them. And ours has vanished on the very night we need it most! Do you have any idea how important the deepest frost is? Of how many people need hope at this time of year? If tonight's frost isn't scattered, then over the course of winter the robin's breast will lose its colour, snowflakes will stop sparkling, holly berries will shrivel and people will forget that Christmas even existed! All the little things that spark joy at this time of year will be lost without the deepest frost. And all those hearts close to breaking will never know the comfort our magic can bring."

Ada chewed her lip. "There's not a moment to lose. I've got to get Upstairs and start scattering magic!"

Mrs Frostgobble clutched her daughter's hand. "We can't let you Upstairs for the first time alone."

Ada squeezed her mother tight. "I won't be alone." She glanced at Bertie. "I'll have him."

Bertie, who had been admiring his silver fingertips, looked up. "My name's Bertie and I really would be very happy to help."

Mrs Frostgobble glanced from Ada to Bertie and then to her husband. "We have to let them go, don't we? We have to trust that the magic knows what it's doing."

Mr Frostgobble sighed. "I fear so. We can't let all that hope slip through our fingers now. Not when so many people need it." He turned to his daughter. "You must be careful, Ada. It's a big, old world Upstairs."

"I am seven, Dad. I am never careful." And with that, Ada hugged her father, grabbed a velvet cape hanging from a branch and charged off through the trees.

Bertie and Mr and Mrs Frostgobble hurried after her.

"Keep her safe," Mrs Frostgobble said when they reached the foot of the stairs.

"And make sure you hold Ada's hand when jumping between the rooftops," Mr Frostgobble urged as his daughter disappeared through the trapdoor with a whoop. "The gap between Number 21 and Number 23 is huge."

"You— you scatter frost from the rooftops?!" Bertie stammered. "I thought we'd just be nipping in and out of people's gardens through secret doors like the one I found earlier!"

"Heavens, no," Mrs Frostgobble replied. "Archibald made that door because of your mother's vegetable patch; he's fond of her rhubarb because, mixed with custard from our cauldron, it makes for a really delicious fudge. But magic – now, that is at its best when unleashed from a height."

Bertie gulped as he ran up the stairs and climbed back through the trapdoor after Ada. He had not thought this through.

Ada, however, didn't look like the kind of goblin who thought anything through. She was smaller than Bertie but she moved at pace, tearing through the kitchen of 35 Muddle Lane before bursting into the garden, gasping and giggling at the moonlit world before her.

"What a place!" she cried. "What a rhubarb-filled wonder of a place!"

A hush had descended over Clatterstomp, Bertie noticed, and the night had thickened. It would be past his bedtime and his family, as he had suspected, appeared not to have realised he was gone. Bertie tried to tell himself this was a good thing as Ada pointed to the boughs of a large vine growing up the front of the house before them.

"That must be the wisteria Mum and Dad climb to get to the rooftops."

Bertie eyed it nervously. "Isn't there a ladder or something nearby?"

"Vines *are* ladders," Ada replied, "just with added danger."

Then she threw herself at the wisteria with such determination that Bertie feared the whole thing would come crashing down. But it didn't. So, very cautiously, he climbed up after her. It was only when they were halfway up the wisteria that Bertie noticed something wriggling in the hood of Ada's cape. To his surprise, the head of a little red squirrel popped out.

"Don't mind Scoff," Ada called down. "He just tags along for the free fudge. Salted caramel is his favourite."

Ada reached into her pocket and drew out a piece. Scoff seized it, swallowed it whole then burped loudly.

"Sorry about that," Ada said. "I'm working on his manners."

They carried on climbing until they reached the roof. Bertie didn't dare look down as he clambered up the slates after Ada. Then they sat, panting, on a chimney pot.

"The world is even more beautiful than I imagined," Ada murmured.

Bertie glanced around. He'd never thought of night-time as being especially interesting but looking at it now, he noticed there was so much he had missed. Rooftops rose into the sky like overturned ships, painted blue by the moonlight. And above them shone a thousand shivering stars. Scoff leapt out of Ada's hood onto her knee. He surveyed the scene, then decided fudge was more interesting than the big, wide world and began poking his nose into Ada's pocket.

Ada handed over a second cube of salted caramel.

"It's so quiet up here," Bertie whispered.
Ada nodded. "Everyone's asleep. It's gone midnight."

"How can you tell?"

"Because it's important." Ada's nose wiggled up and down, then left to right, just as her mother's had done. "We've got a job to do and we've got to do it before dawn. So, my nose is telling me it's already eight minutes past midnight – usually my busiest time of day even without being in charge of the deepest frost."

"What are you busy with?" Bertie asked.

"Adventures mostly." Ada straightened her cape as she readied herself for the task ahead. "Every night, I sit in my hammock and wait for something exciting to happen to me. And by eight minutes past midnight something usually does. Yesterday I rescued a golden bat trapped in a hollow tree and last week a firefly showed me a secret tunnel leading on from our cave." She grabbed Scoff and tucked him into her hood. "I've only ever been adventuring with Scoff before but it's way more fun having you around, too."

Bertie's face lit up. "You really think so?"

Ada stood up. "If this all goes well, shall I sign you up for another adventure next weekend?"

"Yes, please," Bertie replied. "I'd like that very much."

And then he glanced across at 33 Muddle Lane. The lights were off and not a sound could be heard. All of a sudden, Bertie felt his heart wobble. He hadn't wanted his family to notice he was gone but thinking of them all tucked up in bed, having not given him a second thought, touched a familiar nerve.

Ada followed Bertie's gaze. "Your home?"

Bertie nodded.

And Ada, though she was only seven years old – and a goblin, a creature prone to putting its large, hairy feet in delicate situations – wisely replied, "We'll start in the other direction." She yanked Bertie up. "Come on. The night won't last forever and the people of Clatterstomp need the deepest frost."

Bertie looked at his silver fingertips. "But— but— I don't know what to do!"

Ada grinned. "Mum and Dad always tell me frost magic works best if you take a run-up."

Ada hurtled down the length of the roof, with her arms outstretched and her cape billowing behind her.

Bertie watched, open-mouthed, because silver was falling from Ada's fingertips. It started as a little thread winding its way into the night, but as Ada kept running, more and more silver poured from her fingers until she was trailing clouds of glittering ice. And what was left in her wake was nothing short of miraculous: a whole rooftop sparkling with frost.

It was dazzlingly bright. Brighter than the stars. Brighter even than the moon.

Ada laughed and Bertie laughed and then Bertie was running after Ada with his arms outstretched, too, because magic was happening up here on the rooftops.

And when magic happens to a child with
a wobbly heart, it is all the more glorious.

Silver sprung from Bertie's fingertips, coils of it unwinding into the night and settling, as frost, on the grass below and on the leaves and window panes until every surface glistened.

On and on they ran, leaping between rooftops as they scattered the deepest frost. It clung to drainpipes, swirled across windscreens, laced hedges, coated swings and made diamonds of driveways. Nothing was left uncovered. The frost fell everywhere. Even Scoff stopped begging for fudge and looked on, from Ada's hood, in awe.

Eventually, they circled back onto Muddle Lane and sat on the chimney pot on Bertie's own roof. He looked out over the town once again. It was as if a giant had breathed silver into every corner of Clatterstomp, and yet he and Ada had done this. They had created a glittering kingdom and they had done it before dawn. Bertie thought of the frost magic rekindling hope in the sleeping hearts of all those who needed it. And then he sighed. Casting the deepest frost had made him feel so important, but now a familiar emptiness spread out inside him.

"You're sad," Ada said matter-of-factly. She handed Scoff, who was sitting on her knee, yet another piece of fudge. "Very sad."

Bertie shifted. Was his terrible secret – that he didn't belong in his own family – so obvious? "How do you know that?"

Ada's nose wiggled. "Just picking up important things: the time, wobbly hearts."

"I don't think I belong in my family," he said quietly. "I think there might have been a mix-up at the hospital when I was born and I ended up here by mistake. My parents and sisters are all so loud and I'm . . ." Bertie paused, "I'm not. I'm quiet, and in my family being quiet makes you invisible."

Ada was silent for a while. Only Scoff could be heard, chewing fudge. And then he stopped, laid down his treat, flopped off Ada's knee and climbed into Bertie's lap. The squirrel sat there, two little paws resting on Bertie's hands, because he could sense that some things were even more important than fudge.

"Being quiet makes you a good listener," Ada said. "And being a good listener means you hear things most people miss. Like the way you heard my dad sniffing the night – and look where that led you."

"But being a good listener also means you get forgotten about," Bertie said glumly.

Scoff nuzzled against Bertie's tummy and Ada smiled.

"You know what, Bertie? I just don't think you're the forgettable type."

The silence of the night swelled around them until it was beating with a rhythm all of its own. Bertie listened as all the sounds that he had missed before crept a little closer: the flap of a bat's wings; a fox bark; the strange tinkle of faraway stars.

Maybe there is something to be said for quietness after all, Bertie thought.

The frost shone brighter still and then it let the last of its magic loose. Hope tiptoed into Bertie's heart and as this hope stirred inside him, his ears caught on another sound.

Ada heard it, too. So did Scoff, who darted back
inside Ada's hood. It was the faint but undeniable
sound of a group of people shouting. The shouting
grew louder. And louder. Until Bertie and Ada could
hear the word that was being shouted again and again
in panicked voices. It was a name. Bertie's name.

Five figures burst onto Muddle Lane. "Bertie!"
his mum, dad and sisters hollered. "Bertie! Bertie!"

Bertie blinked. His family hadn't gone to bed
and forgotten all about him. They'd been
out looking for him! They cared
about him after all!

Ada chuckled. "I told you, Bertie: you're not the forgettable type."

The Crash-Wallops hurtled down Muddle Lane calling Bertie's name. And all the while, Bertie's heart soared. He belonged!

"I'm here!" he called. "I'm up here!"

One by one, his mother, father and sisters looked up at the rooftop of 33 Muddle Lane.

"Bertie?" his father cried. "On the roof?! Good heavens! Oh, but you haven't run away! We've found you!"

"My darling boy!" his mother exclaimed. "We searched the whole town for you, and the fields and woods beyond, as soon as we realised you weren't at home. But you're here – and you're okay!"

Bertie couldn't believe what he was hearing. "I— I thought you wouldn't notice I was gone."

"Of course we'd notice!" chorused The Hurricane. "You're our brother!"

"Oh, Bertie," his mother sobbed. "We love you so much!"

"And we're sorry if we've not shown you that enough," Bertie's father said. "We're going to make it up to you."

Bertie smiled and the smile went deep inside his heart as the joy of knowing he was loved spread through him. And yet he thought it strange that his family hadn't commented on the goblin beside him, or her greedy squirrel.

He turned to Ada. But she and Scoff were nowhere to be seen. And his fingertips were no longer silver. Only the frost remained, sparkling mischievously back at him.

Bertie wondered many things as he climbed down the wisteria from the roof that night. Had he really met a family of goblins beneath the house next door? Had he and Ada really scattered frost from the rooftops? And would his family still notice him after the deepest frost had gone?

There were answers waiting for Bertie when he woke the next morning. First, a message etched into the frost on his bedroom window:

You never know
what you might find
under the kitchen sink.
Love, Ada.

And next, the sight that greeted him when he walked into the kitchen. His family had risen early and on the table lay a plate of pancakes heaped with blueberries and honey beside a banana milkshake.

Later that morning, the Crash-Wallop family went for a long walk through the woods beyond the town. The frost crunched beneath their boots and though Bertie knew it would melt soon, he knew his family's love for him was here to stay. And he also knew something else: that beneath the kitchen sink next door there were trees made of moonlight, a lake of molten stardust and a little goblin girl who had signed him up for another adventure.